Peter and Susie Find a Family

Peter and Susie Find a Family

Edith Hess

Illustrated by Jacqueline Blass
Translated by Miriam Moore

Abingdon Press
Nashville

Peter and Susie Find a Family

© by Ex Libris Verlag AG, Zürich 1972 and 1981
Translation copyright © 1984 by Abingdon Press

ISBN 0-687-30848-8
Printed in Switzerland

Peter and Susie Find a Family

Mr. and Mrs. Findley lived in a town. They had been married for several years, and they were happy. They had a cozy apartment. Red geraniums bloomed on the balcony. In the living room, an aquarium with a lot of bright fish stood next to many books.

It was a quiet, warm summer evening. Suddenly a baby cried in a neighbor's home. Mrs. Findley stopped her sewing for awhile and thought; Mr. Findley also thought. They thought about the baby because they wanted to have children. Mr. and Mrs. Findley were a little sad.

They only had a dog.

Mr. and Mrs. Findley's dog was called Curly because he had curly hair. Whenever strangers came, he barked as loudly as he could. However, to the children in the neighborhood he was very lovable. He knew them all, and they could pet him as much as they wanted.

Curly liked that a lot. However, what he liked most of all was for Mrs. Findley to take him along on a stroll or a shopping trip. Then he wagged his tail and sometimes barked for joy.

At night Curly slept in a large basket in the kitchen. He scrunched himself cozily down into the soft pillow, stretched out his paws, and fell contentedly asleep.

Mr. and Mrs. Findley had many friends. They often visited with each other. In the summer, Mr. and Mrs. Findley sometimes rode out with their friends, or they put knapsacks on their backs and hiked out into the country.

The nicest thing on such a day was a picnic at the edge of the woods. Curly liked this and naturally the children of the Findley's friends also liked it. They played hide-and-seek, searched for rocks and fruits, and when lunchtime drew near, they collected brushwood for the fire. Mr. Findley cut spears out of small branches, and they all roasted their hot dogs on the fire with them. Everything tasted much better than at home. It's too bad that such a beautiful summer day ends so quickly.

Although everything was going well for them, Mr. and Mrs. Findley were sometimes sad. They wanted a child, and they had been waiting a long time. Again and again they talked about this, and often they imagined how beautiful it would be if a little boy or a little girl lived with them.

One day while they were talking, Mrs. Findley said: "If we can have no child of our own . . ." and Mr. Findley finished the sentence: "Then we could still adopt a child." That night Mr. and Mrs. Findley lay awake. There was so much to talk about and think over.

The next day Mr. and Mrs. Findley went to the adoption agency. There they were greeted by Miss Weber, a social worker. She helped the people who would like to adopt children and helped the children find good parents.

"Miss Weber, we would like to adopt a child who is looking for a father and a mother. We will always provide well for a child. Can you help us?"

"I do not know yet," Miss Weber said. "First, I must find out whether you are the right parents for one of our special children."

Then Miss Weber asked many questions and talked with Mr. and Mrs. Findley for a long time. She wanted to get to know them well.

Mr. Findley said: "We are not rich, but neither are we poor. We could easily provide for a child and buy anything needed."

"We have a room with a little child's bed. We have clothes and shoes, a small bathtub, and a stroller," Mrs. Findley added.

"And also a dog named Curly, with whom our child could play," Mr. Findley said.

"Is that all?" Miss Weber asked.

"Isn't that enough?" Mr. Findley asked. He could not understand why Miss Weber wasn't satisfied.

"No, that is not at all enough. You have forgotten the most important thing." Miss Weber remained steadfast.

But Mrs. Findley knew what she meant. "We will have much love for our child. Of that we can assure you, Miss Weber. If we are allowed to adopt a child, then we will love that child with all our hearts. We want to share our life and love with a child just as we share these with each other."

"That is what I wanted to hear," Miss Weber said. "I think you are the right parents for one of our very special children." Finally, Miss Weber promised to visit the Findleys soon. Then Mr. and Mrs. Findley went home. They were happy that they would soon have a child.

Who are these special children Miss Weber mentioned? Sometimes parents cannot care for their children properly. Perhaps these parents have no home or cannot care for their children themselves. However, because they wanted their children to grow up in a family, some parents give their children to an adoption agency and ask the agency to look for new parents. At the adoption agency, these children are cared for so that they can grow up healthy and happy.

Until the adoption agency finds the right parents, the children are placed in a children's home or in a foster home. Later these children may receive the name of their new parents and stay with them forever. That is called "adoption". Some children come to their new parents when they are still very small, maybe just a few weeks old; others, when they are older and perhaps can even read and write.

After a few days, Miss Weber visited Mr. and Mrs. Findley. She wanted to see where the child would sleep and play. She wanted to know many things and looked closely around the apartment. Satisfied, she finally left. She now knew that Mr. and Mrs. Findley had a cozy home in which a small child would feel happy.

Many weeks passed. Mr. and Mrs. Findley kept waiting for news from Miss Weber. They had almost lost hope. Impatiently, Mrs. Findley called the adoption agency: "Miss Weber, we have been waiting so long for our child! Please don't forget us!"

"There are so many parents who would like to adopt a child. You must still wait a little longer. I'll certainly give you news soon." Miss Weber tried to comfort the impatient Mrs. Findley.

One morning the telephone finally rang. It was Miss Weber. "I have good news for you. We have a small boy who needs new parents. Come tomorrow to the children's home and meet Peter!"

Mr. and Mrs. Findley could scarcely wait. They were at Miss Weber's office early the next day, very excited and full of joy.

Next, Miss Weber told them everything important about Peter and his first parents. "If you are not completely certain you want to be the parents of this child, let me know," Miss Weber said.
Then she finally went with Mr. and Mrs. Findley to the children's home.

The boy was lying in a little white bed and was sleeping. He appeared rosy and fat. Suddenly he opened his big brown eyes and smiled.

Mrs. Findley leaned over him: "This little boy could be our child?" Then she soft- ly stroked his little head. After awhile, she said to her husband: "I think we will love him very much. What do you think?"

Mr. Findley laughed and said: "Yes, we have always wanted a little boy just like this one. We want to get everything ready for little Peter. When can we take him home?"

"I hope in a few days," Miss Weber answered.

The Findleys were happy that at last they had found a child they could care for. Peter smiled at his new parents and kicked his little legs.

That same day, Mr. and Mrs. Findley went shopping and bought bottles, diapers, powder, a soft hairbrush, and everything else a baby needs. After a few days, Peter arrived in his new home. Mrs. Findley gave him something to drink, wrapped him gently, and placed him in his little bed. Soon Peter fell asleep.

Mr. and Mrs. Findley, however, stood for a long time at his little bed and were happy. They didn't notice that Curly slipped in and sniffed around everywhere. He seemed to like little Peter because he wagged his tail.

Two weeks passed. Then Mr. and Mrs. Findley thought it was time to invite relatives and friends over. And they all came—the new grandparents, the uncles and aunts with their children, and, of course, the friends of Mr. and Mrs. Findley. Little Peter became excited and astonished when they brought him many bright toys as welcome gifts. There was a small yellow duck among the gifts. Every day it would float around in the bathtub when Mrs. Findley bathed Peter.

Peter grew rapidly and was soon so big that he could crawl, walk, climb, and speak. He liked to play hide-and-seek with his daddy best of all. Then he hid behind the curtains and bookcases and loved it when no one could find him. However, when it was Daddy's turn to hide, Peter always knew where to find him.

In the summer Mrs. Findley often went with Peter to the playground. There was a slide there, and monkey bars, a sandbox, and many other children.

One time there was a bigger boy at the playground who always bothered the smaller children. He fussed with Peter and tried to pull the sandpail out of Peter's hand. But Peter wouldn't let this happen and shouted out loud: "Mother!"

The big boy made fun of him: "That isn't your mother. You are only an adopted child."

Peter was confused for a moment. Then he shouted back: "I want you to know I am a very special child. My parents chose me out of hundreds of children. Don't you think that means they love me?"

The big boy grew quiet. He left Peter and the other children alone.

Peter liked best of all to play with a little girl who had freckles on her nose and blonde pigtails. When evening came and he had to go home, Peter was always a little sad, for at home, he was completely alone with his parents. Still, he didn't tell anyone that he would like to have a little sister. However, his parents sensed his wish, and since they also wanted another child, they asked Peter one day: "Would you like to have a little sister to play with? What do you think? Should we adopt a little girl?"

Peter hesitated and said: "I don't know— I want to think about it."

That evening Peter couldn't go to sleep for a long time. He thought: A real little sister would really be something. Would Mother and Daddy still love me? However, Peter knew his parents loved him very much, and a little sister to play with would be fun.

The next morning he ran into the bedroom of his parents and shouted: "I have thought it over. You can bring home my little sister today."

"It doesn't work that quickly, Peter," Mother said. "But we will ask Miss Weber first thing tomorrow whether she can help us."

Again Mr. and Mrs. Findley went to the adoption agency. Peter went along. Miss Weber scarcely recognized him, now that Peter had become such a big boy.

"Would you like to have a little sister?" Miss Weber asked.

"Yes," Peter answered. "Then I'll get a big bed, and my little sister may sleep in my baby bed. If she wants, I'll give her my toys to play with."

"That is so nice of you," Miss Weber said. "Then I shall look for a little sister for you. But you must have a lot of patience, because there are many parents who also want to adopt a child."

Several months went by. Peter and his parents almost believed that Miss Weber had forgotten them. One day the phone rang. Miss Weber had good news. She said, "I have found a little girl. Her name is Susie. Susie could perhaps become Peter's little sister. Do you want to go with me to the children's home tomorrow?"

A pleasant little girl waited for Peter and his parents in the children's home. She smiled at all three. Then Susie stretched out her hand, grasped Peter's finger, and wouldn't let go. Peter liked Susie. Then Mrs. Findley took the little girl in her arms and held her protectively.

Peter asked, "May we take Susie with us, Miss Weber?"

Because Miss Weber knew the Findleys and knew that they could be trusted with a child, everything went somewhat faster.

The next Sunday, Susie went home with her new parents and new brother.

Again there was a big party with cake, lemonade, and tea. All the grandparents, the uncles, aunts, children, and friends of the family came to greet Susie.

All admired her little snub nose and her lively brown curls. However, Peter was also praised by everyone as he brought out his works of art with Curly.

"Dear God, please see to it that Susie grows up quickly so she can play with me," Peter prayed every evening when he lay down in his new bed. He could not understand why Susie was still so small, and sometimes he thought: If only I had a bigger little sister.

However, when Peter was allowed to help Mother feed Susie, change her, or bathe her in a little tub, then he felt very proud to be Susie's big brother. Every Sunday the Findleys went for a walk with their two children. Susie sat in a baby carriage, and Peter led Curly, who, of course, wanted to go along. From time to time Mr. and Mrs. Findley looked at each other and smiled. They were happy that they had children.

SUGGESTIONS FOR PARENTS AND EDUCATORS

Children will find *Peter and Susie Find a Family* exciting and will enjoy the bright pictures that highlight the book. They will want to hear again and again about Peter and Susie, as they become more caught up in the story of the two adopted children.

Because the children will read and react to the story of Peter and Susie as a beautiful picture book, they will need no instruction in finding the book's deeper meaning. The instruction is aimed at the grown-ups. Most adoptive parents know how important it is to tell their children about their backgrounds, since keeping these backgrounds a secret could be harmful. However, some adoptive parents are uncertain how and when they should tell their children about adoption, and this book could help these parents. Some parents might read this story to their children and then explain how the children were adopted in a similar way to Peter and Susie. Other parents may prefer to substitute their own family names and experiences in the story. Others will show their children only the pictures and use their own words.

Four-year-old children can understand the story of Peter and Susie. However, they won't be able to understand everything the first time. Therefore, it is good to repeat the story. When adopted children grow older, they will probably want to know the specific circumstances of their own adoption. It is best for parents to answer as many questions as possible. They should speak with respect and understanding for the birth parents, who perhaps went through much pain so that their children would grow up in a harmonious family life. Some adoptive parents are afraid their children will pull away from them when they hear the truth, but these parents will learn that such fears are unfounded. Indeed, the feeling of togetherness usually becomes stronger. The earlier the explanation is given, the more naturally it is accepted by the children and becomes a part of them. Children told too late or not at all sometimes hold bitter resentment against their adoptive parents.

Not only children who are adopted, as Peter and Susie are, but all children should learn what adoption is. In our society there are more and more adoptive children. Everyone should know that these children

live with their parents contentedly and in a harmonious way, just like the children who grow up with their
birth parents. Then when children meet adopted
children in kindergarten or in the early school years,
there won't be any problems.